W9-DHW-840

This book belongs to

_____

 An Early Start Edition from Macmillan Children's Book Clubs

THE WONDERFUL FEAST

By Esphyr Slobodkina

 GREENWILLOW BOOKS, New York

Early in the morning
Farmer Jones got up.
He stretched himself
and said,

"It is, indeed,
a beautiful morning.
The sun is shining bright,

the corn has grown tall,
the birds are singing fine,
and I feel fine too!"

Then he went into the shed
and gave his horse a great
big measure of feed.

"My," said the
old horse, Spotty.
"What a wonderful
feast I'm going
to have!"

He ate all he wanted
and went to sleep.

Then everything was quiet again,

and

nothing was heard but the sleepy sighs of Spotty.

While
Spotty slept,
little she-goat
Nanny wandered
into the shed.

She looked
at what was left
of Spotty's meal
and said,
"My, oh, my!
What a wonderful
feast I'm going
to have!"

She ate all she wanted and
wandered out of the shed.

Just then

the red hen,
Strawberry, walked in,
looking for her breakfast.
"Children, children," she called.
"Look what a wonderful
feast we are going
to have!"

In a moment the floor was covered with little yellow chicks, and there was a great noise and commotion while they had their meal.

But all was quiet again in the shed after they left.

"Oh, my—
oh, my—
oh, my!"

whispered a little mouse,
peeping out of his hole.
"What a wonderful feast
I'm going to have!"

He quickly crossed the
floor where the few scattered grains lay
and took all he could to his house.

And then a busy
old ant crawled in,
searching for
winter supplies.

He picked up the last grain
and carried it away,
muttering all the time to himself,

**"My, oh, my!
What a wonderful feast I'm going to have!"**

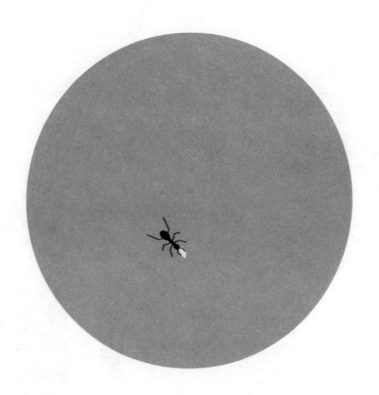

Copyright 1955 by Lothrop, Lee & Shepard Co., Inc.
First published in 1955 by Lothrop, Lee & Shepard
Co., Inc. New, revised edition published in
1993 by Greenwillow Books. All rights
reserved. No part of this book may be repro-
duced or utilized in any form or by any means,
electronic or mechanical, including photo-
copying, recording, or by any information
storage and retrieval system, without permis-
sion in writing from the Publisher, Greenwillow
Books, a division of William Morrow &
Company, Inc., 1350 Avenue of the Americas,
New York, NY 10019.
Printed in the United States of America
First Edition   10 9 8 7 6 5 4 3 2 1

Library of Congress Cataloging-in-Publication Data
Slobodkina, Esphyr (date)
The Wonderful Feast / by Esphyr Slobodkina.—
New, rev. ed.
    p.   cm.
Summary: Farmer Jones feeds his horse
a wonderful feast, and from what is left
a number of other animals also have
a wonderful feast.
ISBN 0-688-12348-1.
ISBN 0-688-12349-X (lib. bdg.)
[1. Domestic animals—Fiction.]
I. Title.
[PZ7.S6334Wo   1993]
[E]—dc20
92-23416   CIP   AC